CONTENTS

Amanda Pig
and the Wiggly Tooth

A Puffin Easy-to-Read

by Jean Van Leeuwen
pictures by Ann Schweninger

PUFFIN BOOKS

To Liz, a pearl of a girl,
and The Tooth Fairy (you know who you are)
–J.V.L.

For my dear friend, Jane Bicks
–A.S.

PUFFIN BOOKS
Published by the Penguin Group
Penguin Young Readers Group,
345 Hudson Street, New York, New York 10014, U.S.A.
Penguin Group (Canada), 90 Eglinton Avenue East, Suite 700, Toronto, Ontario, Canada M4P 2Y3
(a division of Pearson Penguin Canada Inc.)
Penguin Books Ltd, 80 Strand, London WC2R 0RL, England
Penguin Ireland, 25 St Stephen's Green, Dublin 2, Ireland (a division of Penguin Books Ltd)
Penguin Group (Australia), 250 Camberwell Road, Camberwell, Victoria 3124, Australia
(a division of Pearson Australia Group Pty Ltd)
Penguin Books India Pvt Ltd, 11 Community Centre, Panchsheel Park, New Delhi - 110 017, India
Penguin Group (NZ), 67 Apollo Drive, Rosedale, North Shore 0632, New Zealand
(a division of Pearson New Zealand Ltd.)
Penguin Books (South Africa) (Pty) Ltd, 24 Sturdee Avenue, Rosebank, Johannesburg 2196, South Africa

Registered Offices: Penguin Books Ltd, 80 Strand, London WC2R 0RL, England

First published in the United States of America by Dial, a division of Penguin Young Readers Group, 2008
Published by Puffin Books, a division of Penguin Young Readers Group, 2009

1 3 5 7 9 10 8 6 4 2

Text copyright © Jean Van Leeuwen, 2008
Pictures copyright © Ann Schweninger, 2008
All rights reserved
THE LIBRARY OF CONGRESS HAS CATALOGED THE DIAL EDITION AS FOLLOWS:
Van Leeuwen, Jean.
Amanda Pig and the wiggly tooth / Jean Van Leeuwen; pictures by Ann Schweninger.
p. cm.
Summary: When Amanda Pig has her first loose tooth, she is reluctant to pull it.
ISBN 978-0-8037-3104-2 (hc)
[1.Teeth—Fiction. 2. Pigs—Fiction.] I. Schweninger, Ann, ill. II. Title.
PZ7.V3273Anm 2008
[E]—dc22 2005028224

Puffin Books ISBN 978-0-14-241290-9

The full-color artwork was prepared using carbon pencil, colored pencils, and watercolor washes.

Puffin® and Easy-to-Read® are registered trademarks of Penguin Group (USA) Inc.

Printed in China

Reading Level 1.9

The Wiggly Tooth

Amanda took a great big bite

of her peanut butter sandwich.

Something moved in her mouth.

"My tooth!" she said.

"It's all wiggly."

She wiggled it

up and down and sideways.

"Look," she said.

"I have a loose tooth!"

"You're lucky," said her friend Lollipop.

"I wish I had one."

"That's nothing," said William.

"I have two."

He wiggled his two front teeth.

"I lost two already," said Sam. "See?"

"You look like my baby sister,"

said Lollipop.

It was fun having a loose tooth.

Amanda told everyone.

"Look," she said to the music teacher.

"I have a loose tooth!"

"How nice," said the music teacher.

"Now let's sing."

He started playing the piano.

"Amanda," he said. "You're not singing."

"Oh," said Amanda. "I forgot.

I was wiggling my loose tooth."

"Look," she said at recess.

"I have a loose tooth!"

"Great," said Lily. "Want to jump rope?"

"Sure," said Amanda.

   She wiggled her tooth while she jumped.

"Let's climb on the monkey bars,"

   said Lollipop.

"Okay," said Amanda.

   She wiggled her tooth upside down.

"Look," she said to her teacher.

"I have a loose tooth!"

"Super!" said Mrs. Mary Ann Pig.

"Soon the Tooth Fairy will come

to your house.

But now it's time for reading."

Lily read out loud.

Spencer read out loud.

"Amanda, it's your turn,"

 said Mrs. Mary Ann Pig.

"What are you doing?"

"Um," said Amanda. "Wiggling my tooth."

She wiggled it during math.

"Amanda," said Mrs. Mary Ann Pig.

"You're not counting."

She wiggled it during drawing.

"Amanda," said Mrs. Mary Ann Pig.

"You need to get to work
on your picture of spring."

Finally Amanda got to work.

Everyone held up their pictures.

"Oh, my!" said Mrs. Mary Ann Pig.

"I like all your flowers and birds
and blue skies and rainbows.
And William's frog.
And Amanda, what a beautiful mountain!"

"That's not a mountain," said Amanda.

"It's my tooth."

To Pull or Not to Pull

"Look," said Amanda.

"I have a loose tooth!"

"Your very first one," said Mother.

"Let me see," said Father.

Amanda wiggled her tooth.

"It's really loose," said Oliver.

"Shall we pull it out?" asked Father.

Amanda thought about it.

"Will it hurt?" she asked.

"No," said Father.

"Maybe a little," said Mother.

"It might bleed," said Oliver.

"A whole lot."

"No!" said Amanda. "Don't pull it out."

"Okay," said Father.

"We will wait for it to fall out."

Amanda waited.

She wiggled her tooth

up and down and sideways.

She jiggled it.

But it did not fall out.

"You better not eat that apple,"

said Mother.

"Or that cookie," said Oliver.

"Or that corn on the cob."

Apples and cookies and corn on the cob

were Amanda's best foods.

Now all she could eat

every day

was peanut butter.

Amanda got tired of peanut butter.

Having a loose tooth

wasn't fun anymore.

"Okay," she said.

"You can pull out my tooth."

Father took her to the bathroom.

He sat her on a high stool.

"Are you ready?" he asked.

Amanda took a deep breath.

"I will count to three," said Father,

"and your tooth will be gone.

One. Two—"

"Wait!" said Amanda.

"I need Sallie Rabbit."

She ran to her room

and got Sallie Rabbit.

"Now I am ready," she said.

"Here we go," said Father.

"One. Two—"

"Wait!" said Amanda.

"I need Susie and Sophie too."

She ran to her room

and got Susie and Sophie Rabbit.

She hugged them all tight.

"Ready," she said.

"One," said Father. "Two—"

"Wait!" said Amanda.

"Will it really hurt and bleed?"

"Maybe a tiny bit," said Father.

"But you are brave.

   Just close your eyes

   and think of nice things."

Amanda closed her eyes.

She thought of flowers and birds.

She thought of blue skies and rainbows.

"Ready," she said.

"One," said Father. "Two—"

She thought of hurting and bleeding.

"Wait!" said Amanda.

"I don't want you to pull out my tooth."

A Surprise

Amanda's tooth would not fall out.

She wiggled it

up and down and sideways.

She jiggled it.

She twirled it around in a circle.

But it did not fall out.

"Will my tooth ever come out?" she asked.

"Don't think about it," said Mother.

"And someday

you will have a nice surprise."

The next day

Amanda did not think about her tooth.

She went to school

and had peanut butter for lunch

and came home and played with Lollipop.

"How is my little Tooth Girl?"

asked Father at dinner time.

Amanda smiled.

"Your tooth!" said Father. "It's gone!"

Amanda felt in her mouth.

There was a great big empty space

where her tooth used to be.

"But where is it?" she asked.

She looked everywhere.

In her pocket and her jacket

and her lunch box and her book bag.

But Amanda could not find her tooth.

She felt like crying.

"I need it to put under my pillow

so the Tooth Fairy will come," she said.

"I will help you," said Oliver.

"Did you have your tooth at school?"

"Yes," said Amanda.

"I wiggled it once in reading.

And once on the bus."

"Aha!" said Oliver.

"My great detective brain says

you lost it after school.

What did you and Lollipop do?"

"Played dress-up with our rabbits

and rode bikes and played ball,"

said Amanda.

"Follow me," said Oliver.

They looked all over Amanda's room.

In the dress-up box and on the floor

and under her bed.

"No tooth," said Amanda.

"But thanks for cleaning up."

They looked outside on the road.

"I see it!" said Amanda.

"Oh, no. It's only a pebble."

"I see lots of pebbles," said Oliver.

"But no tooth."

They looked in the front yard.

"Too much grass," said Amanda.

They crawled through the grass.

"I see a worm," said Oliver.

"And a spider web. But no tooth."

"I give up!" said Amanda.

"I'll never find my tooth."

At bedtime, Amanda said,

"My tooth is lost forever.

Now the Tooth Fairy won't come."

She started to cry.

"I think she will," said Mother.

"No," said Amanda.

"You have to leave your tooth."

She hugged Sallie Rabbit.

All of a sudden,

something fell out of Sallie's ear.

"My tooth!" said Amanda.

"How did it get there?" said Mother.

"I don't know," said Amanda.

"But thank you, Sallie Rabbit!"

The Tooth Fairy

Amanda wrote a letter to the Tooth Fairy.

Dear Tooth Fairy,

This is the very first tooth I lost.

It really was lost, but then I found it.

Please leave me some money.

Thank you.   Love, Amanda

PS: What do you do with all the teeth?

Amanda put her tooth

and the letter under her pillow.

"Good night, Amanda," said Mother.

"Good night," said Amanda.

She closed her eyes.

She was almost asleep.

Then she thought,

"What if the Tooth Fairy doesn't know

where to look for my tooth?"

Amanda got up.

She made a sign.

She put it on her door

and got back into bed.

She closed her eyes.

She was almost asleep.

Then she thought,

"What if the Tooth Fairy doesn't know

how to read?

I better stay awake

so I can show her my tooth."

Amanda waited for the Tooth Fairy.

She heard a sound outside her door.

"Tooth Fairy?" she said.

No one answered.

"It must be Mother and Father

going to their room," she thought.

Amanda waited some more.

She heard a little noise in her closet.

"Tooth Fairy?" she said.

No one answered.

What would the Tooth Fairy

be doing in her closet?

Maybe it was a monster.

"No!" she said.

"There are no such things as monsters."

Amanda waited some more.

She was getting sleepy.

Her eyes kept closing.

She heard a tiny noise outside.

It sounded like fairy wings.

"Tooth Fairy?" she said.

No one answered.

"It was only a breeze," she thought.

"Maybe the Tooth Fairy isn't coming.

Maybe she got lost."

Amanda's eyes closed.

In the morning

she looked under her pillow.

"My tooth is gone!" she said.

In its place was money and a note.

Dear Amanda,

What a beautiful tooth! Please send more.

Love, Your Tooth Fairy.

PS: I save the teeth. I must have a million.

Amanda felt in her mouth.

Next to her empty space

something wiggled.

"Mother!" she called.

Mother came running.

"Look," said Amanda.

"I have a loose tooth!"